Pig and Cat Are Pals

Douglas Florian

I Like to Read®

HOLIDAY HOUSE • NEW YORK

I LIKE TO READ is a registered trademark of Holiday House Publishing, Inc.

Copyright © 2018 by Douglas Florian
All Rights Reserved
HOLIDAY HOUSE is registered in the U.S. Patent and Trademark Office.
Printed and bound in November 2017 at Tien Wah Press, Johor Bahru, Johor, Malaysia.
The artwork was created with crayon and colored pencil on manila paper.
www.holidayhouse.com
First Edition
1 3 5 7 9 10 8 6 4 2

Library of Congress Cataloging-in-Publication Data is available.

ISBN 978-0-8234-3858-7 (hardcover)
ISBN 978-0-8234-3938-6 (paperback)

Pig and Cat are pals.

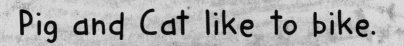

Pig and Cat like to bike.

Now the neighborhood seems so quiet.

Will I ever have a best friend again?

My best friend and I knew
each other when we were babies.

We started kindergarten,

and grade school together.

But then she moved away. Now I will
have to go to school all by myself.

My best friend and I always had
so much fun hanging out in our fort,

exploring new galaxies,

or playing soccer.

But then she moved away. Now I will
be bored for the rest of my life.

My best friend and I sometimes got in fights,

but we always made up.

Now that she moved away I
have no one to say I'm sorry to.

My best friend and I shared everything, like secrets,

Halloween candy, and even

the chicken pox!

Now that she moved away, who will I share things with?

A new family is moving into my best friend's house.

They have a dog . . .

and toys . . .

and someone who looks my age!

My best friend moved away,

and I'm sure going to miss her.

But I know she'll make new friends—
just like me!